For **Mom** and **Dad**,
thanks for all your support and
for teaching me how to make pizza.

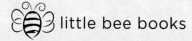

little bee books

A division of Bonnier Publishing
853 Broadway, New York, New York 10003
Copyright © 2016 by Claire Lordon
All rights reserved, including the right of reproduction in whole or in part in any form.
LITTLE BEE BOOKS is a trademark of Bonnier Publishing Group, and associated colophon
is a trademark of Bonnier Publishing Group.
Manufactured in China   LEO 0516
First Edition
2 4 6 8 10 9 7 5 3 1
Library of Congress Cataloging-in-Publication Data is available upon request.
ISBN 978-1-4998-0228-3

littlebeebooks.com
bonnierpublishing.com

LORENZO
THE PIZZA-LOVING LOBSTER

by Claire Lordon

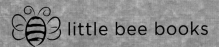

little bee books

Lorenzo was an adventurous lobster who loved discovering new foods and exploring fun places.

One day as he was walking on the beach,
he came across a seagull eating from a paper plate.

"What's that?" asked Lorenzo.
"It smells **amazing**!"

"This is called pizza.
Would you like to try some?"
the seagull asked.

Lorenzo took a small bite,
pausing to taste the flavors.
Then he had a **big** bite.

Pizza?
This is so tasty!

Lorenzo ate the rest of the delicious pizza and treasured every bite.

He thanked the seagull and
rushed home to tell his friends.

The friends started collecting items to make the pizza.

Lorenzo and Kalena put their pizza creation in the oven.

DING!

This isn't quite right.

Kalena slowly chewed on her piece.

Maybe it had kelp dough, squid ink, algae, and coral rings?

Let's try that!

I remember now! It was

sponge patties,

jellyfish jelly,

seaweed noodles,

and seashells!

Are you sure?

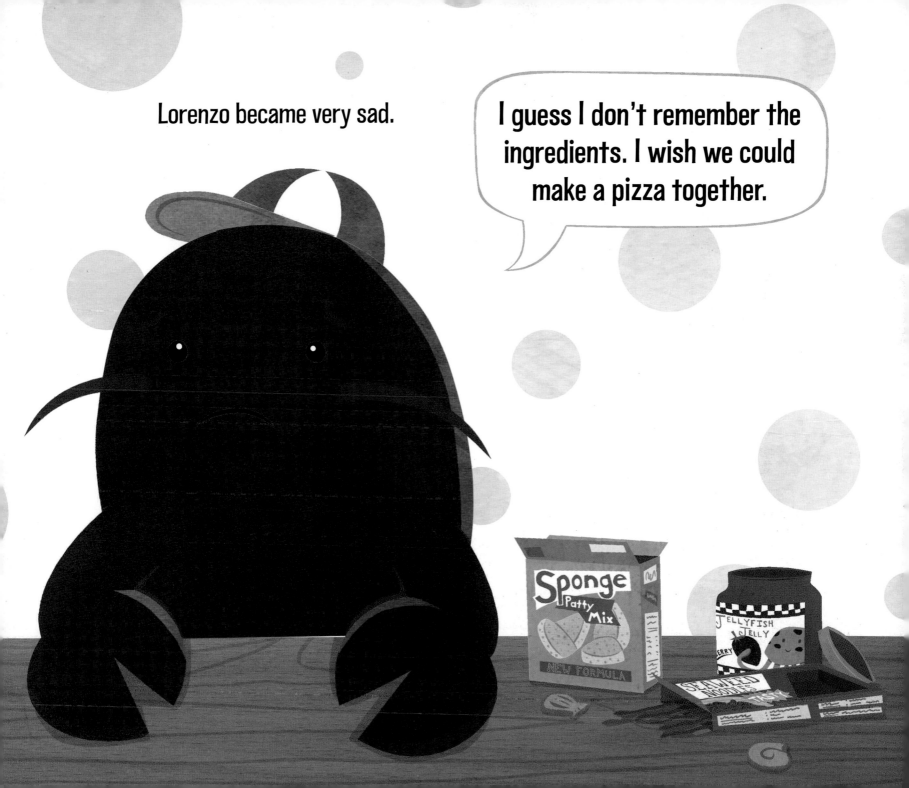

A very hungry Kalena left Lorenzo's house.
She was upset with the awful food Lorenzo fed her.

Pizza must be really bad, she thought.

Kalena returned to find Lorenzo moping in his backyard.

Hey Lorenzo, look what I found!

Lorenzo looked at the food and took a bite.

Holy anchovy! This is exactly like the pizza I had earlier, but this time it's big and round!

The two friends closely studied the pizza...

...and had a big pizza party with all their friends!

PARTY

Pin the Pepperoni